DECIDE & SURVIVE™

THE ATTACK ON PEARL HARBOR

Published by Milk & Cookies, an imprint of Bushel & Peck Books. Bushel & Peck Books
is a family-run publishing house in Fresno, California, that believes in uplifting children
with the highest standards of art, music, literature, and ideas. Find beautiful books for
gifted young minds at www.bushelandpeckbooks.com.

Type set in LTC Kennerley Pro and Bobby Jones.
Graphic elements licensed from Shutterstock.com.

Bushel & Peck Books is dedicated to fighting illiteracy all over the world.
For every book we sell, we donate one to a child in need—book for book.
To nominate a school or an organization to receive free books,
please visit www.bushelandpeckbooks.com.

LCCN: TK
ISBN: 978-1-63819-179-7

First Edition

Printed in the United States

1 3 5 7 9 10 8 6 4 2

THE ATTACK ON PEARL HARBOR

CAN YOU STOP THE ASSAULT?

JARRET KEENE | MIKE ANDERSON

MILK +
COOKIES

YOUR CALL TO ADVENTURE!

Dear Reader, this is *your* story. *You* control how history happens through the choices you make.

Don't read this book from the first page to the last. Instead, follow the directions at the bottom of each page. When you're offered options, choose wisely because your decision could end in disaster as easily as triumph.

No matter how your tale ends, feel free to start over and create a different one with a new outcome.

Adventure, mystery, danger, and fortune await. Good luck!

BACKSTORY

December 7, 1941: Your father is a naval medical officer stationed at the Pearl Harbor Navy Yard on O'ahu, Territory of Hawaii. Life is sweet for you and your sister Beatrice: swimming in the pool at the base, taking field trips with classmates on warships, and meeting actress Shirley Temple at your sister's birthday party. It turns out you and Temple are close in age!

War looms on the horizon. But for the most part, despite being on high alert as Japan and Germany build up their militaries, your family savors their time in the paradise of a Pacific archipelago. Blue water. Warm sun all year round. Beaches with white, red, green, and black sand! It's a beautiful, exotic landscape. You can't imagine how it could be better.

Well, except for getting comic books faster. Sometimes it takes the commissary months to put the latest issue of Action Comics starring Superman on the spinner rack. At least you and your best friend, Marvin, can catch the latest radio episodes of *The Shadow*.

Sometimes you imagine yourself a hero in your own adventure movie serial. A hero like Tarzan or the Phantom. The tropical rainforests of the Big Island provide the background for a thrilling jungle film. You and Marvin are always exploring, bicycling, fishing, riding horses, hunting banana moth caterpillars with sharp sticks, and learning to surf the waves. You also like hanging out with Jenny, a classmate at school. She is funny and brave, and you like playing baseball with her. She's a strong pitcher who throws you excellent speedballs. You like playing catcher because you can see the entire field—diamond, outfield, and spectators.

You're in excellent condition as a result of living on an island. When things take a frightening turn, you're ready to run, hide, and fight. On a beautiful Sunday morning, the Imperial Japanese Navy begins bombing the U.S. base. With explosions all around, there is a blood-chilling rumor: The Japanese have launched a land invasion.

Will you search for your father amidst the burning ships of the naval yard? Or stay and shield your mother from razor-sharp bayonets?

There's an additional challenge. Your annoying yet devoted sister refuses to leave your side. Do you bring her along or risk putting your sibling in harm's way?

It's time to decide and survive!

➲ **BEGIN YOUR ADVENTURE ON THE NEXT PAGE.**

YOUR ADVENTURE
BEGINS

Your dad is somewhere on patrol this morning. You're throwing a baseball back and forth with your friend Marvin in the front yard of his parents' bungalow. Marvin isn't an athlete, but he is a devoted friend. You like Marvin. And you love this neighborhood. It's located along the shoreline of Battleship Row, where the USS *Arizona* and USS *West Virginia* are moored.

It's early in the morning. Your mother is frying bacon for Sunday breakfast. Your sister is sleeping, having stayed up late reading a book: *Black Beauty* by Anna Sewell. It's about horses. You want to read it, but you'll never admit it.

Marvin's mom is planting butterhead lettuce for the spring season. His father is a doctor, too, delivering an officer's baby at the hospital.

You hear the engines before you see them: a formation of low-flying torpedo planes, grazing the tops of palm trees. Nothing unusual, a typical morning.

You raise your hand to wave, but something is wrong.

Very wrong. The aircraft are khaki-colored with red

circles under their wings.

"Look!" says Marvin to his mother, who is outside gardening. "Torpedo planes!"

She gets up from the flower bed and stares skyward. She stands stock-still under an onslaught of planes. Her expression is anguished, terrified. She drops her spade.

"Those are not ours. Everyone inside, please!"

Japanese fighter planes!

➲ **GO TO PAGE 24.**

You wave at the pilot. He waves back warily, then continues punching the glass. He doesn't have much time: Water fills the cockpit. He's close to drowning. You think: He won't attack someone trying to save him, right?

As the prow of your boat bumps the plane's nose, you see the problem. A piece of torqued metal caused by crash impact has snagged the window. You use the end of your wooden oar to break off the jagged debris. With a crunching sound, it comes loose.

It takes all your strength to help the pilot open the cockpit window. He leaps out, his goggles making him look like a space alien, and stumbles onto the wet sand. You lead him up the beach. Suddenly, you feel something clenched against your neck.

The pilot has his parachute cord around your throat.

Before you black out, you hear the sound of the slingshot: THWIP. The pilot yelps, and the pressure on your throat disappears. Your sister Beatrice has blasted a ball bearing into the pilot's goggles, shattering them. He struggles to remove them.

You grab a nearby banyan branch and wallop him. The pilot collapses into the surf, knocked unconscious.

"You're welcome," Beatrice says.

Then a zero plane strafes the beach. Your sister falls

to the ground, grazed on her arm by a bullet. It's not even close to fatal, but there is blood.

"Take me to the house," she says, tears on her face from the pain. "And find Dad."

➲ **GO TO PAGE 38.**

You notice there's a field telephone system sitting in its leather case next to the radio. You pick up the handset and hand-crank the battery. Your friend Marvin's dad showed you how to do this once. Will anyone be listening?

It ends up being the commander of the USS *Breese*, a destroyer! Despite the chatter of guns in the background, Commander Taupin says that he sees your father's ship, the USS *Ramsay*, starboard side.

"The ship doesn't appear hit," he says. "It's firing its guns at Japanese bombers!"

This is great news! But wait . . . Why is your father warning of a land invasion if he's on board the *Ramsay*?

"Commander Taupin," you say. "Can you see my dad from where you are?"

"No," he says, "And I haven't heard him on the radio. If there is a land invasion, you need to make sure that enough sailors know about it. The assault must be repelled!"

"Yes, sir," you say with a gulp.

You can't mess around. You must get the manual to the men trying to rescue people trapped inside the USS *Oklahoma*. This is a critical decision.

➲ YOU DON'T WANT TO SEND MARVIN ALONE. DO YOU FIND A GROWN-UP TO DELIVER THE MANUAL, AND THEN HEAD IMMEDIATELY TO THE BEACH TO FIGHT THE INVADERS? IF SO, GO TO PAGE 90.

➲ DO YOU DELIVER THE MAP YOURSELF AND THEN HEAD TO WAIKIKI BEACH? IF SO, GO TO PAGE 52.

The PT boat cuts its engine. Your father puts on a life vest and settles into a dinghy to meet you ashore. You notice that he's wearing a holstered pistol. You've never seen it on him before. It doesn't give you a good feeling. Your glad he's the one wearing it.

You and Marvin greet him at the waterline. When he steps out of the dinghy, he seems taller than you remember.

"Dad!" you say with relief, hugging him tightly.

He returns the embrace. "You made it all the way here? I'm proud of you, son."

"Dr. Bramley!" Marvin says. (Everyone calls him Dr. Bramley. You call him Dad.) "Is there really an invasion?"

"Friendly fire is causing confusion," he explains. "Antiaircraft shells landing all over the island have spooked everyone. Now we hear word of Japanese parachutists. We're heading out to investigate."

"Can we come?" asks Marvin.

"Beatrice is hurt," you tell your father.

His voice is serious, "How bad?"

"I don't know," you say.

Dr. Bramley studies your face, then looks back at the PT boat. He's quiet for a moment. Then he says, "Can you administer medicine to Beatrice?"

You've never given her more than a spoonful of castor oil.

➲ **TO GO BACK TO THE HOUSE AND TREAT YOUR SISTER, GO TO PAGE 102.**

➲ **IF YOU CONVINCE YOUR FATHER TO COME WITH YOU TO CHECK ON YOUR SISTER, GO TO PAGE 64.**

➲ **IF YOU JOIN YOUR FATHER IN ADDRESSING THE IMMEDIATE THREAT OF INVASION, GO TO PAGE 77.**

You and your friends are terrible at stealth. Your attempt to sneak past the enemy fails. You end up getting cornered beside a waterfall.

The paratrooper isn't Japanese. He's not even a paratrooper.

You instead find yourself face to face with a sailor in the U.S. Navy.

His face isn't familiar.

How did he get here?

➲ **GO TO PAGE 48.**

Henry picks the lock and enters the shed. It's hot inside. You use your flashlight to illuminate the space.

You gasp in horror.

You're not an enlisted sailor in the navy, but you know a bomb when you see one. It's not an explosive made in the U.S., either. There's Japanese writing stenciled on the weapon. This object isn't made to thwart Imperial subs. It's designed to kill Americans.

"For a minute, I trusted you, Harry," you say. "If that's even your real name."

His face is completely different now. Cold and calculating.

He charges. Though he's bigger than you, he slips on a palm frond. You're able to use some of the Judo you've learned on the island. You use his weight and momentum to throw him into a tree. He cracks his head hard against the trunk.

"Ouch," he says, dazed from the impact.

⮕ **IF YOU TAKE ADVANTAGE OF THE SITUATION TO GRAB HIS WALLET AND LOCKPICK, GO TO PAGE 99.**

⮕ **IF YOU TAKE OFF RUNNING, GO TO PAGE 39.**

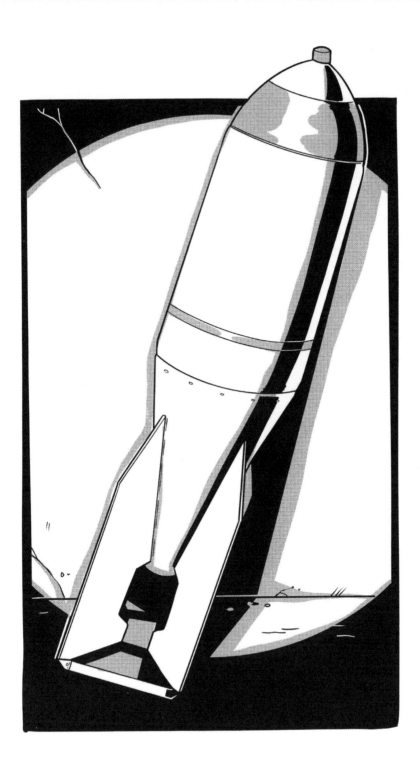

You lose your opportunity to catch your family's abductors. Your mother and sister are held for ransom by Imperial Japan. You don't know if you'll ever see them again.

Your father is heartbroken. Jenny and the Kimura twins feel sad for you.

THE END

You immediately start to doubt the wisdom of handing over your classmates to a shellshocked bunch of sailors. They just watched their friends die in an attack. What good will come from presenting them with half-Japanese Americans?

"This is a dumb idea," you announce.

They look at you with fear in their eyes. But also trust. You are a natural leader, and they have faith in your decision-making.

It's better to show how American everyone is by putting a plan into action.

➲ **GO TO PAGE 98.**

You run to your own house, next door to Marvin's. You have to warn your mother and sister.

They must've heard Marvin's mom screaming, because they already know. Pearl Harbor is under attack.

"Get into the fireplace," your mother insists, grabbing your arm.

You don't see your sister in the living room.

You hear the sound of machine guns.

➲ **IF YOU JOIN YOUR MOTHER IN THE FIREPLACE, GO TO PAGE 36.**

➲ **IF YOU YANK FREE TO FIND YOUR SISTER, GO TO PAGE 54.**

Beatrice doesn't like it, but she agrees to take care of your mother while you search for Dad.

Before you can leave, the house catches fire from loose wiring caused by all the damage. Your mother clings desperately to your sister, pleading with you not to leave. She begs you to grab the garden hose and put out the flames.

She doesn't have to ask again. It's your family.

You dart into the front yard and turn on the water. Then you drag the hose into the house. The curtains are burning. It's a big, bright-orange blaze. You concentrate the water there.

After you douse the curtains, the fire is out. You go from room to room, looking for patches of flame to extinguish.

Bullets strafe the back yard again, shattering the tire swing hanging from the mango tree. You flatten yourself on the ground, praying you don't get hit.

The noise is frightening, drywall dust everywhere. You wait a moment before standing up.

A chunk of masonry landed on your sister's head. She's a brave girl, refusing to cry. But you see the pain in her face. Blood is streaming.

If only your dad, a medical doctor, was here. You do your best with the first aid kit your dad gave you when the family relocated to Pearl Harbor. You apply iodine and gauze, but Beatrice needs stitches. You don't feel qualified.

She seems a little out of it. You worry she might have a concussion. It's imperative now: You must find your father.

➲ **GO TO PAGE 38.**

The cockpit glass smashes apart into fragments. This causes more water to rush into the plane. The aircraft begins to sink.

The pilot, shielding his head with his arms, seems concerned that you'll crack his head with the anchor. Instead, you toss it into the water, and it lands with a splash.

You reach your hand through the shattered glass and tap him on the shoulder. He looks up and unfastens his seat straps. You help the pilot open the cockpit window.

As he steps out of the plane, he grabs you by the shirt, HARD. The two of you tumble into the water. Before you get your bearings, you feel the weight of a grown man pushing your head below the surface. You're being drowned.

Suddenly the pilot relents. You spring out of the water, gasping for air. You see your sister smiling proudly with the anchor in her hand. She used it to clobber the pilot.

But then the waves cause the plane to shift. Your sister loses her balance. She knocks her head against the propeller, opening a gash. She's bleeding.

"I'm heading back to the house," she screams at you.

"Beatrice, wait," you say. "I have the first aid kit."

She waves you away. "Grab your bike and find Dad."

➲ **GO TO PAGE 38.**

Amazingly, you find a third bicycle, abandoned in a patch of grass. The three of you pedal back to Ford Island, searching for a radio along the way. You need to warn the admiral. There are Japanese soldiers invading Oahu's East Shore!

A police station comes into view along the main road. The office is unlocked. Your father immediately takes a seat at the desk and dials a number.

The switchboard is chaos, but after a few more attempts he gets through. The admiral is alerted

Air support is called in. Minutes later, heading back to Ford Island, you hear the bombs falling on the enemy.

Stopped in time. You and your father, and perhaps even Marvin, might be celebrated as heroes at the end of this battle.

That is, if the U.S. wins.

THE END

The four of you run along the beach in the direction of the jetty. Your hunch was correct. You find your father and two dozen university ROTC students digging trenches.

"Dad!" you say. "Can we help?"

Elated to see you, he rushes to embrace you, then gives you an update. A landing ship is nearly here, threading the waterway between the beach and the Diamond Head volcanic formation.

"I have to ask you to undertake a mission," he says, looking grave. "It could be dangerous."

"I have my friends," you say. "Maybe they can join me."

He nods. "We have unconfirmed reports of paratroopers landing in Manoa Valley. I need you to scout the area and confirm the intel."

Whatever you do, you're not to engage the enemy. If the information is true, your father and the U.S. Navy have big problems.

There's no radio for you to use. You'll have to scan the area and return quickly.

➲ **THE KIMURA TWINS SPEAK FLUENT JAPANESE. IF YOU DECIDE TO TAKE THEM WITH YOU TO SEARCH FOR THE ENEMY IN MANOA VALLEY, GO TO PAGE 61.**

➲ YOU ALWAYS WORK BEST ON YOUR OWN. IF YOU ATTEMPT THE MISSION ALONE, GO TO PAGE 80.

➲ IF YOU ONLY ASK JENNY, WHO YOU SUSPECT HAS CRUSH ON YOU, TO RIDE ALONG, TURN TO PAGE 46.

You bicycle back to your family home, and along the way you reunite with Jenny and the Kimura twins.

Your dad was right. No one is home.

"Let's check the hospital," Jenny says.

"Won't it be overrun?" Dan Kimura asks.

You squat on your haunches to examine the beach sand in your front yard. "There's no chance they're in the hospital."

Jenny furrows her brow. "What makes you say that?"

You point to the multiple, messy boot prints. A struggle took place here.

"My family has been abducted," you say.

➲ TO FOLLOW THE BOOT TRACKS TO SEE WHERE THEY LEAD, GO TO PAGE 96.

➲ IF YOU WAIT TO FILE A MISSING-PERSONS REPORT WITH LOCAL LAW ENFORCEMENT, GO TO PAGE 22.

It's better to split up anyway. You run hard for a few minutes. You spot a dark cave near a noisy waterfall and decide to take your chances. You hope the sound of rushing water covers up any noises you make.

The cave is empty and cool. You crouch in the shade and look out at the water.

You see something that makes you clutch your chest.

You dropped your flashlight in the creek bed. Anyone walking by will know someone is here.

You run to retrieve it. That's when he sees you.

A sailor in the U.S. Navy.

➲ **GO TO PAGE 48.**

You're a hero! You delay the plane from flying off with your mother and sister. You hinder the kidnappers long enough for the military police to show up and rescue your family.

U.S. military officers handcuff the perpetrators. They're enemy pilots who parachuted onto the island hours after the attack began!

Your father has arrived by this time, thrilled that his family is safe. "They didn't count on this kid!" he says.

He playfully messes up your hair.

It feels good to be a secret hero of the Pearl Harbor attack.

THE END

You jump in the fireplace with your mother, leaving your sister to fend for herself in her bedroom.

The chaos is unreal. Bullets riddle the house. A wall collapses, but the roof holds. A fire starts, ignited by loose electric wires.

After putting out the blaze with a garden hose, you spend the rest of the morning cowering in fear. You wait to hear from your father in your singed, smoky home.

He isn't located until many hours later.

Your sister remains missing.

Will she ever be found?

THE END

With your sister hurt, you spring into action. You run to the front yard, where your bicycle leans against the side of the house. You check the bike for damage. It seems fine, so off you go in search of the only person you trust to treat your sister's wound.

The noise of detonations rattles your teeth as you pedal bravely toward the chaos. You hear voices shouting from PA systems on board the ships as they catch fire and burn. So many bombs falling now in the bright morning sun that they resemble glittering snowflakes.

You get about 100 yards in the direction of the ships when you brake hard. You clutch your chest in horror as you witness the *Oklahoma* slowly roll over on her side. She flips until her mast begins to scrape below the waterline and against the mud of the harbor. The ship looks like a dead whale turning over to die.

You hear the men screaming inside. There is no way you can help them by yourself.

Your buddy Marvin suddenly pulls up next to you on his bike. It's good to see him.

"We have to help," he says.

⮑ **GO TO PAGE 55.**

You take off running, but not before grabbing Henry's wallet.

"Come back!" he screams.

You don't stop to answer. You crash through the jungle. You must reach the beach before Henry grabs you and hands you over to the enemy.

You don't want to be captured by those responsible for a heinous attack. You know many Japanese people here on the island. They are kind and generous. They love America. Like Jenny and the Kimura twins.

Henry's behavior is suspicious.

Time to find out who he really is.

➲ **GO TO PAGE 57.**

You and Marvin race toward the fire department. It is, ironically, on fire. Water spews from a bombed water main.

Bodies of the fire crew lie in the grass. For a moment, you think they're sleeping. Or playing possum.

Marvin is shocked, rubbing his eyes. He doesn't look so good.

You see Commander Owens pushing a hose wagon toward the shipyard. He sprays the structure with water pumped from the beach. You leap from your bicycle, waving at him to stop.

"Sir," you say. "Men are trapped inside the *Oklahoma*. There's a rescue effort, but they're concerned about hitting a fuel tank."

The officer stops spraying the building and looks at you. He narrows his eyes and scoffs. Then he drops the hose and stomps toward the burning structure.

"Commander Owens?" you say.

You follow behind him a few paces until he reaches a file cabinet. It's steaming from the heat of the fire. The commander knocks it over with a hard boot kick. Folders spill out, documents scatter. Pulling a handkerchief from his pocket, he uses it to fish out a map.

"Take this," he says. "Say, you look familiar. You the doctor's son?"

You nod and seal the map inside your backpack. Suddenly, there's a blinding flash. You're thrown backward. You're unscathed, but groggy, numb. You get back up.

Commander Owens has survived, but only briefly. You see him lying in black smoke, his leg shattered.

Dying, he mumbles for a tourniquet.

Your friend Marvin approaches. He says in your still-ringing ear: "I—I don't think a tourniquet will help. We should go."

➲ **IF YOU ATTEMPT TO SEARCH FOR SOMETHING THAT MIGHT WORK AS A TOURNIQUET, GO TO PAGE 58.**

➲ **IF YOU ABANDON COMMANDER OWENS AND TAKE THE MANUAL TO THE USS *OKLAHOMA*, GO TO PAGE 74.**

You head out with your buddy Marvin to find Commander Taupin. It takes you nearly an hour to reach Ford Island.

By this time, the naval base is chaotic from rescue efforts. Smoke is everywhere. And there are so many people yelling at each other for help.

You see the destroyer and rush to locate the commander.

A sailor suddenly stands in your way. "Young man," he says. Seawater-drenched, he uses a rag to wipe oil from his white uniform. "You shouldn't be here. Go to your family."

"I need to find Commander Taupin. They're invading at Waikiki."

His eyebrows shoot up in alarm. "Follow me."

He leads you to the harbor, where several officers have gathered. You can tell they're focused on rescue efforts. The sailor salutes Commander Taupin, who now looks at you.

You reflexively gulp for air.

He approaches. As you salute, he swats at the air, indicating that you stop. "Tell me," he says, "about the invasion."

"My father and I saw them," you say. "We barely escaped."

He nods. "We'll dispatch two destroyers and a PT boat."

You breathe a sigh of relief. But only for a moment.

"In the meantime," the commander continues, "I need you to grab a map of the USS *Oklahoma* from the ruined fire-department substation. We don't know how to reach the men trapped inside the Oklahoma without hitting a fuel tank and blowing up the ship!"

➲ **YOU DON'T REALLY HAVE A CHOICE, SO DO YOU LEAVE RIGHT NOW FOR THE MAP? IF SO, GO TO PAGE 90.**

➲ **OR DO YOU WANT TO DELIVER THE MAP TO THE USS *OKLAHOMA* YOURSELF AND THEN HEAD TOWARD WAIKIKI BEACH? IF THIS IS YOUR DECISION, GO TO PAGE 105.**

You launch Jenny's kite into the air, letting the wind grab it high above the tree line. You tether the string to a tree next to a small rounded cliff face above a cave entrance. You stomp your shoes into the dirt outside the cave, leaving footprints.

Then you scale the rock to reach the top of the bluff. You, Jenny, and the Kimura twins hide behind a sizable boulder . . . and you wait.

Soon, you hear the crunch of military boots. Imperial troopers emerge from the foliage. They inspect the string before noticing footprints leading to the cave.

From your elevated height, you see your father on the beach. He has with him with several ROTC university students. He sees the Japanese sub. You sense that he plans to wreck it. Instead, he starts digging trenches.

One of the soldiers below snaps on a flashlight. He waves his colleagues into the darkness, leading them into the cave.

That's when the four of you, grunting hard, push the boulder off the bluff, sealing the entrance below. The Japanese soldiers are trapped.

Then you all start running back to the beach. It seems you should help your father dig trenches in preparation for more enemy soldiers.

 **GO TO PAGE 29.**

Sometimes it's better to work alone. Jenny is a great athlete and fast on a bicycle. Trying to impress you, she pedals too far ahead and is captured by Imperial pilots.

You start to head back, but it's too late. You're surrounded, and now your father has no way of knowing. Soon he will be captured, too.

THE END

The sailor's name is Henry, and he's from California. Together the two of you survey the southern perimeter of Manoa Valley. You find no evidence of an invading army. What you think is a parachute is really an old tent flap that the wind swept into the trees.

Was it all a false alarm? Maybe the enemy is good at hiding tracks.

"I don't see anything," says Henry. "Do you?"

You shake your head.

"OK, let's check the beach," he says.

You agree. Your father is digging trenches in preparation for a land invasion.

The two of you make your way back to the water.

You're relieved you didn't find Japanese soldiers. But what if you missed them?

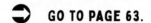 **GO TO PAGE 63.**

Holy wow! You and Marvin pedaled for nearly an hour to reach Waikiki Beach. Near the shoreline, you hear gunfire. You ditch your bicycles to tiptoe closer to the firefight. Crouching behind some koa trees, you see your father, alone, pinned down behind a skiff boat.

A Japanese sub is on the shore, soldiers emerging. They aim at the skiff, splintering it with bullets.

Your dad returns fire with a pistol. It does little to slow the enemy.

You pull the flare gun from your backpack, point it straight up in the air, and squeeze the trigger.

A dazzling orange-yellow ball of fire soars into the heavens. The soldiers look up, distracted.

That's when your father tosses a smoke grenade at them.

The enemy begins choking on purple smoke.

Your dad runs toward you smiling. He joins you and Marvin in racing away from the beach.

"We must alert the sailors," your dad says. "Can you find Commander Taupin on the USS *Breese*? His destroyer ship is intact."

Remember: This is your dear father asking you to save the day. But you only just now found him after a long search. Shouldn't you bring him home to treat your sister? Maybe he'll give you medicine to take to Beatrice.

Then again, he's the only one brave enough to stand in the way. You can't let him fight alone.

➲ **IF YOU HEAD TOWARD FORD ISLAND TO ALERT THE USS *BREESE*, GO TO PAGE 43.**

➲ **IF YOU CONVINCE YOUR FATHER TO GIVE YOU MEDICINE TO BRING TO YOUR SISTER, GO TO PAGE 102.**

You try to respond to your father on the radio, but you don't know how to work the equipment. You give up when you see the radio's operational platform is damaged.

You have enough info to go on. Your dad is on the beach, waiting to meet an invasion. He knows something big is coming. He needs help.

"Well," says Marvin. "What are we waiting for?"

You're not a fighter. Just a kid. Are you strong enough to join the strongest person you know in fighting enemy pilots?

➲ DO YOU WANT TO SPEND MORE TIME TRYING TO CONTACT YOUR FATHER? IF SO, GO TO PAGE 15.

➲ WANT TO HEAD TO THE USS *OKLAHOMA* WITH THE SHIP MANUAL? GO TO PAGE 89.

➲ DITCH THE MANUAL, AND HEAD TO WAIKIKI BEACH TO THWART AN INVASION? GO TO PAGE 49.

You secure the map and decide to take on the added responsibility of delivering it to the ship. When you and Marvin finally reach the rescue crew working to save sailors trapped inside the USS *Oklahoma*, the attack reaches a crescendo.

Bullets are flying. Bombs are exploding everywhere.

There's so much noise and chaos that you don't even feel the shrapnel that hits you.

THE END

You use the time machine to go back to 1890s-era Germany. You find work as babysitter for a family, and you spend a lot of time caring for their son.

You teach the boy about the importance of love and affection. You save his baby brother from a terrible bout of measles by keeping him hydrated and comfortable. You encourage the boy to look beyond someone's ethnicity and race to see their value and humanity.

One night, when the parents are at a party, you stand above the boy while he is sleeping.

You take a pillow from his bed.

And you place it under his tired head, so that he is comfortable.

The boy's name is Adolph.

You do everything you can to make a him a good person to avoid the bloody conflict that is World War II.

To avoid the Holocaust.

Hiroshima.

Pearl Harbor.

THE END

You pull loose from your mother's grasp, frantically searching for Beatrice.

You find her in her bedroom at the exact moment that a spray of bullets slams into the wall above her sleeping head. She bolts upright and turns to see the bullet holes.

Had she been sitting on her bed instead of lying down, she'd be dead.

She looks at you with panic and tries to scream. But there's no noise.

"You're OK," you say. "We're getting out of this."

➲ TO TELL BEATRICE TO COME WITH YOU. YOU MUST LEAVE THE BUNGALOWS TO FIND YOUR FATHER. GO TO PAGE 65.

➲ TO TELL HER TO JOIN YOUR MOTHER AND TRY TO REACH YOUR FATHER ON THE PHONE. GO TO PAGE 25.

Japanese pilots strafe Ford Island. The sound of bullets hitting everything—trees, water, dirt—is ghastly.

You and Marvin use clusters of palm trees for cover. You see three maintenance crewmembers, Hawaii natives, running into the water. They carry blowtorches and pneumatic chippers. It looks like they plan to cut and burn their way through the ship's hull to rescue the men trapped inside. The rescuers scamper on top of the capsized *Oklahoma*.

Your father doesn't always stick to the same ship during a shift. What if he's trapped inside?

"Can we help?" you yell out to the maintenance men.

One of them looks at you and Marvin, nearly losing the chipper as it starts to slide off the ship's metal keel. Finally, he says, "You can keep our equipment from falling into the water. Get up here, both of you!"

You and Marvin drop your bikes on the shore, drenching your shoes and clothes as the men reach down to pull you onto the overturned ship. You flinch from the loud pop of gunfire.

A young Marine with a rifle stands at the end of a nearby dock, blasting planes in the sky. "If only my parents could see me now," he says, reloading.

The blowtorch technique doesn't work. Flame

causes the paint on the hull to catch fire. The men hand you the torch and switch to an air hammer. Now their efforts are more successful, but it's slow going. The tapping of dozens of men trapped in the ship's belly is eerie. You can't see them, but you imagine them gasping and swimming toward air pockets. You imagine them struggling to orient themselves in an upside-down battleship. They begin using wrenches to bang out an SOS—"Save Our Souls"—in morse code.

It dawns on the rescuers that they don't know exactly what's under the hull. They might be hammering into a fuel tank. Or a powder magazine.

"We need a manual," says the man with the rivet gun. He looks at you. "Find Commander Owens and ask for a map of the Oklahoma. Without it, we risk blowing up survivors and injuring ourselves in the process."

You look at Marvin. Marvin looks at you, eyes wide.

To follow this order means delaying your sister's medical assistance. And your father still hasn't been found.

 **GO TO PAGE 86.**

In his wallet, you find a hand-drawn map of the island. It's dotted with X's.

One of the X's is where he claimed the torpedo launcher is located.

What's inside the shed might not be what he said it is.

⮎ **TURN TO PAGE 88.**

You run inside the wrecked station. You search everywhere for something to stop the bleeding.

"Hey," Marvin insists. "Get out of there!"

Zero fighter planes strafe the structure.

With you inside it.

THE END

You're exhausted by the time you reach the edge of Waikiki Beach.

You hear voices in the distance, so you hide your bike under a clutch of palm fronds.

You stay quiet and listen. The voices aren't speaking English. It's Japanese.

You keep listening and notice that only two—no, make that three—people are talking. It doesn't sound like a mass of troops. Is it trio of crashed pilots?

You have no weapons, just a flare gun in your backpack.

As the voices get closer, they sound familiar. It's Jenny and two other Nisei students, the Kimura twins, from school! They're coming back from flying kites on the beach.

You step out of the underbrush and into the path. "Jenny?" you say.

The three of them stop, standing stock-still. But why?

Jenny asks, anxious, "You alone?"

"Yes," you say. "Anyone hurt?"

"No," she says. "We're hiding."

"From who?"

"The U.S. Navy. They'll put us in prison."

"Why?"

"For being half-Japanese. If you haven't noticed, Pearl Harbor is under attack."

Jenny and the Kimura brothers are American citizens, born on U.S. territory. Still, could what she says be true?

Why are they here, in the location of a rumored invasion?

➲ **TO GO HELP THEM FIND A PLACE TO HIDE AND AVOID JAIL, GO TO PAGE 98.**

➲ **TO CONVINCE THEM TO TURN THEMSELVES IN TO THE AUTHORITIES, GO TO PAGE 23.**

Outside of P.E. class, you haven't spent much time with the Jenny and the Kimura twins. You know they're excellent football players, even if they never say much. You hope their silence at this moment doesn't mean they're afraid.

You're plenty fearful on your own.

As you make your way deeper into the valley, you notice a hacked pathway. You see evidence of machete strikes in this part of the jungle. You get confirmation that a pilot has landed when a chute, snagged on a tree, billows in the wind.

"They're here," you say quietly.

Jenny and the Kimura twins nod their heads. You hear the pilot walking into the ravine. You peer down and observe, though you can't get a clear view. You know what he's thinking, though. He believes he has the element of surprise. He believes this side of Oahu is his now.

Dan Kimura emits a quiet gasp and points up at the elevated trail.

A policeman makes his way from the other side, obviously investigating the report of paratroopers landing on the island.

➲ DO YOU FIRE A SIGNAL FLARE INTO THE SKY, HOPING TO LURE THE ENEMY AWAY FROM THE POLICE OFFICER? IF SO, TURN TO PAGE 95.

➲ DO YOU AND YOUR FRIENDS SNEAK PAST THE IMPERIAL PILOT TO WARN THE POLICE OFFICER? IF SO, GO TO PAGE 19.

With the help of ROTC university students, your dad builds a sandbag defense of the jetty. You introduce him to Henry. Your father shakes the sailor's hand and tells him to dig trenches.

Your dad gives you a look. He doesn't trust the sailor either. You worry that you've brought a traitor into your midst! Maybe it's better to keep a spy close.

Anyhow, it felt good to be with Jenny and the Kimura twins. You make a mental note to spend more time with them at school. If Oahu isn't taken over by the Japanese, that is.

A buzzing from the sky makes you think about running. But then you see four Curtiss P-40B Tomahawk fighter planes. Friendlies.

"See anything?" you dad asks, indicating the water.

Your dad gives you binoculars to scan. Seabirds. Waves.

Then you see dark shapes making their way toward the beach. They don't look like whales.

"Yes," you say.

➥ **GO TO PAGE 71.**

Imperial pilots catch you before you even leave the jetty.

Your father tries to explain that he is a doctor, not a combat leader. They promise to treat him and his son fairly. And they do. Your career as a Pearl Harbor defender is over.

You hope that your sister isn't hurt badly, that she and your mother remain safe. You hope the others will succeed in driving the enemy out of Oahu.

THE END

"My shoes," she says. "Let me find them."

She's wearing floral pajamas, but she slips on socks and hiking boots anyway.

More gunfire, then a whistling sound.

You run to the window in time to see the USS *Arizona* explode. The detonation rocks the foundation of your house. You fall backward on your tailbone. A shelf displaying your sister's archery awards hits the ground.

"Beatrice," you say, trembling. "Do you still have the slingshot dad gave you for your birthday?"

"Yes," she says.

She leaps off the bed and scampers to her closet to fetch it. She also grabs a crumpled paper bag full of ball bearings. "We need a map of the island," she says. "Got one?"

You sprint into your own room and tear the map from the wall. You stuff it into your knapsack. You get your first aid kit, too.

"Ready," you say, huffing back into your sister's room. For some reason, she puts on a fishing vest littered with metal hooks and lures over her pajamas.

"Me too."

"Let's go," you say.

➲ **GO TO PAGE 84.**

You and Marvin hop on your bicycles and pedal to the white sand of Waikiki Beach. The sun is yellow. The sky is blue with no enemy bombers. The second wave of the attack is over. Is it the last?

Are more bombers coming?

You're sweating. Your mind is overrun with scary facts.

Your sister is wounded.

Your father is missing.

Your mother is worried sick.

And here you are, pedaling all over a naval base and fighting to stay alive.

You hear a plane buzzing and immediately steer your bike under a tree canopy.

It's a Curtiss P-40, a U.S. combat fighter.

"One of ours, yay!" says Marvin, pumping his fist.

You cheer on the pilot even though you have no idea where he's going or what he's doing.

It feels good to see American airpower again.

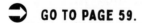 **GO TO PAGE 59.**

"Let him drown," Beatrice says. "We have to find Dad."

"Sis, the Boy Scout motto says to always help others."

"This guy wants you dead!" she says. "No motto on earth says you must help someone kill you."

You notice a whaleboat beneath a nearby coconut tree.

"That'll work," you say.

"I can't believe this," Beatrice groans.

A loud explosion from Battleship Row makes both of you lose your footing for a second.

"Come on," you say.

The two of you head to the whaleboat. You drag it across the sand while Beatrice pushes. Soon you have the vessel in the water. You paddle your way to the plane. There's oil in the water from the bombed battleships. You pray that you don't see a dead body floating anywhere.

Now the pilot makes a fist, slamming the glass in an effort to escape.

"What if he has a gun?" Beatrice says.

"You have a point," you say. "Ready with your slingshot?"

"Yes."

"Good."

Beatrice sighs, indicating that you're a hopeless case.

➲ TO HELP THE ENEMY PILOT SLIDE OPEN THE COCKPIT WINDOW, GO TO PAGE 12.

➲ TO SMASH THE GLASS WITH THE IRON ANCHOR TETHERED TO THE WHALEBOAT, GO TO PAGE 27.

Your dad manages to get a radio working. He lets the Tomahawk fighter planes in the air know what's happening: there are enemy submarines 500 yards from shore.

Under their wings, the planes have no bombs, no depth charges. How will they neutralize the submarines?

"There's a land-based torpedo launcher," says Henry. "It's in an ammo dump not far from here."

Your dad looks at you. "Go with Henry. Bring it here."

You're off and running with the sailor. You trust him.

But not completely.

➲ **GO TO PAGE 82.**

The four of you barely fit in the small boat with an outboard motor. You can't risk leaving someone behind. You'll need all the help you can get.

When you reach the peninsula, you exit the skiff and follow the tracks again. The tents are all empty. You push into the jungle.

The Kimura twins find a military car with keys in the ignition.

"Anyone know how to drive?" Jenny asks.

The four of you look at one another.

Eventually, you get behind the wheel, having never driven anything other than a bicycle. You go bumping and lurching down an uneven road. Your friends scan the forest for your family.

"There!" says Jenny, pointing to a Kawasaki Ki-56, a Japanese two-engine light transport plane. Parked on a runway, its engines suddenly sputter to life. Your mother and sister are being shipped to Japan right in front of your eyes!

"Stop!" you say.

➲ IF YOU TRY TO BLOCK THE PLANE WITH YOUR CAR ON THE RUNWAY TO KEEP IT FROM TAKING OFF, GO TO PAGE 34.

➲ IF YOU YANK YOUR FAMILY OFF THE PLANE BEFORE IT WHEELS DOWN THE RUNWAY, GO TO PAGE 87.

Commander Owens doesn't make it. His death demoralizes you. You start to weep.

Marvin places his hand on your shoulder and says, "We keep going."

You wipe your face with your shirt. It's true. Not all is lost. You haven't found your father. But you do have the manual. It's the key to rescuing sailors trapped inside the USS *Oklahoma*.

Back on your bikes, you and Marvin are about to pedal toward the naval yard. But then you hear static crackling.

It's coming from a radio inside the station's smoking ruins.

"Wait," you say to Marvin.

You put on headphones and listen. Sounds of mayhem. A voice cuts above the noise to announce:

"Attention! The Imperial Japanese Navy is landing on Waikiki Beach. This is a full-scale invasion. Repeat: A full-scale invasion is underway on Waikiki Beach near the jetty."

You recognize the voice.

It's your father's.

➲ **GO TO PAGE 51.**

Henry knows what you plan to do before you can act. He knocks the branch from your hand and pushes you to the ground.

It doesn't hurt, but the embarrassment is painful.

"Too bad you didn't figure it out sooner," Henry says, tying you to a nearby tree.

He activates the timer on the bomb and heads back in the direction of Ford Island.

All you can do is listen to the ticking of the bomb.

THE END

Your classmates Jenny and the Kimura twins arrive on their bikes. They are hiding from U.S. Navy personnel because they are half-Japanese. After the attack on Pearl Harbor, they worry they will be seen as the enemy.

They know you and your father, however. They're safe here.

How will they feel about being asked defend the island from an invasion?

"We're ready," Jenny says. Her voice is brave compared to yours.

The Kimura twins never talk much. Instead, they nod.

Your dad stops digging a trench and approaches. "These your friends?" he asks you.

"Yes," you say, making introductions.

"It's a good thing you're here," your father says. "There are reports of paratroopers in Manoa Valley. I hate to ask this of you, but it's an emergency."

"You want us to scout the area?" you ask.

He nods. "Confirm the intel. Everyone's scared right now. Hopefully, it's nothing. If you see the enemy approach, don't engage. Come straight back here. Stay alert!"

Jenny is the first to respond. "You got it, Dr. Bramley."

He salutes. The four of you snap to attention and salute back.

 **GO TO PAGE 61.**

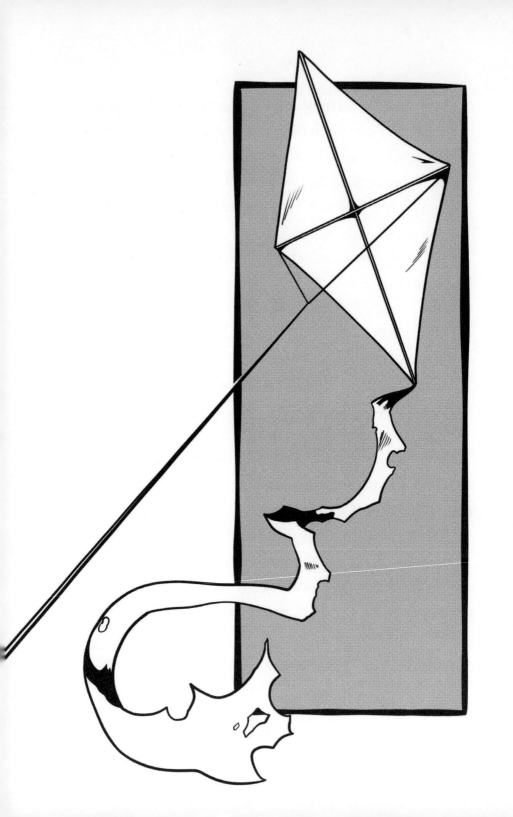

You tear a few pieces from Dan Kimura's red T-shirt. You use the sewing kit in your backpack to attach scraps of the fabric to the kite tail.

"Red means emergency," says Jenny. "I get it now."

You nod and finish the task of creating a distress signal.

In a few minutes, you have the kite airborne. Its tail is a long, scarlet warning, fluttering in the wind like an angry snake tongue.

A squadron of U.S. Navy fighters spots your improvised signal and come swooping down.

They begin strafing an amphibious tank that you hadn't noticed was storming the beach. The vehicle begins to smoke before sputtering to a halt.

"Nick of time!" Jenny cheers.

The Kimura brothers grab you for a double-bear hug, nearly crushing you!

"OK, I think more tanks are coming," you say. "Let's find my dad!"

➲ **GO TO PAGE 29.**

Quietly, you sneak your way into Manoa Valley. The sun is bright in the sky, but the valley is darkened by trees. You keep checking them for snagged enemy parachutes. It feels like dense jungle on this part of the island.

You hear a nearby noise, like rushing water. You determine it's the waterfall you explored here last summer. But then a twig snaps. Someone grabbed a drink and is heading your way.

It's a sailor, an American. He's alone.

You figure he's one of the good guys. You don't avoid him.

"Hey, there," he says, eyes wide. "Where did you come from?"

You don't say anything. At first.

"What's your name?"

You ignore his question. "Why are you hiding?" you ask. "The Japanese attacked the naval base. You should be helping."

"I was putting out fires," the sailor says. He indicates his smudged uniform. "But then I heard the enemy was invading the beach. So I hopped into a vehicle. Lost control and hit a tree."

You don't say anything to this. What about the parachute that you and the Kimura twins saw?

"I mean, I could say the same about you, young man."

He has a point. Can you trust him?

➲ **GO TO PAGE 48.**

Henry leads you to a storage shed and ammo dump next to some tennis courts. There's a padlock.

"Too bad," you say. "A torpedo launcher would be useful."

Henry pulls some items from his pocket: his wallet and a lockpick.

Hey, how did Henry know where a torpedo launcher was stored on this side of the island?

And why does he have a lockpick? Only burglars or people working for the U.S. Office of Strategic Services have this tool.

➲ **IF YOU ACCUSE HIM OF BEING A SABOTEUR FOR IMPERIAL JAPAN, GO TO PAGE 93.**

➲ **IF YOU CONTINUE TO HELP HIM SECURE THE TORPEDO LAUNCHER, GO TO PAGE 20.**

➲ **IF YOU PICK UP A FALLEN TREE LIMB TO KNOCK HENRY UNCONSCIOUS, GO TO PAGE 76.**

You make it to the house. Marvin checks on his family. The air attack seems to be over, but a land invasion is possibly happening. Thankfully, your sister is doing much better.

Your mom has made Beatrice comfortable on the sofa. She's already back to reading a Jane Austen novel!

"How can you read at a time like this?" you ask.

She shrugs and puts away the book. "It calms my nerves," she says with a smile. "Tell me . . . did you find Dad?"

You nod. "Sort of. I know where he is. Heard him on the radio."

Your mom seems aggravated. She pulls at her hair. "Please find him and bring him home."

"Leaving now," you say.

"Be careful, brother," Beatrice says.

"Shucks, Sis," you say. "You really do care about me!"

She playfully tries to punch your arm. The strain makes her clutch her bandaged head. "Oof," she says.

"Stay still," you say. "Try to heal. I'll bring back Dad."

She smiles and gives you a thumbs-up.

You run outside and jump on your bike. You've never pedaled so hard in your life.

➲ **GO TO PAGE 59.**

You take a quick mental inventory of the items you've gathered. Then you grab your sister's arm.

"First, we find dad," you tell her.

The two of you hurriedly exit the house, leaving your mother in the kitchen. You hear her sobbing over the clicking sound of the rotary phone. The emergency numbers are busy.

You and Beatrice stand in the front yard. The sky is crowded with enemy aircraft now. It's a scary spectacle. Pearl Harbor is in flames! The sight causes the hairs on the back of your neck to stand up. In the distance you see the USS *Helm*, a destroyer, launch a torpedo.

You feel the impact in your guts. Judging by the sizzling bubbles, you realize that a Japanese submarine has been blasted. The good guys got one!

"Hurray!" you say.

"Nazis had it coming," Beatrice says.

"Hush," you say. "Imperial Japan is attacking us."

"For now," she snaps back.

You nod. There's work to do. Should you risk your sister's life searching the harbor for your father?

"It's too dangerous," you say. "One of us stays with mom."

"You're not leaving me," she says. "Besides, you need someone who can shoot."

"That's a slingshot," you say.

She shrugs. "Better than nothing."

OK, but the question remains: What should you do?

➲ **TO CONTINUE WITH BEATRICE, GO TO PAGE 101.**

➲ **TO URGE HER TO STAY PUT AND PROTECT YOUR
MOTHER, GO TO PAGE 25.**

"Where do I find Commander Owens?" you ask, hand-ing the torch to a sailor.

"He's at the base fire department," says the crewmember.

You look at Marvin. He knows where that is.

You and Marvin jump from the ship, landing in the shallow water with a splash. The uneven sand causes your ankle to roll. You shake off the pain and limp toward the tower.

"You OK?" Marvin asks.

"Yes," you say. "But I wish Jenny was with us."

"Me, too. Wow, I'm thirsty."

Marvin pulls the canteen off his bike and tosses it at you. You catch it and take a long swig. The water is cold and clean. You feel better already, even if your ankle is throbbing.

"Think the commander has a map of the ship?"

"I hope so," you say. "I hope my father isn't trapped inside this ship."

Marvin tries to console you. "It's not his ship. He's never worked on this one."

"True, but sometimes he fills in for other doctors."

Your buddy nods.

You limp to your bike and pedal toward the fire station. You do your best to keep up with Marvin.

⮌ **GO TO PAGE 40.**

Without so much as a driver's license, you steer the car right up to the plane. Because you're not a great driver—or even an experienced one—you step out of the vehicle without shifting into park.

The car rolls forward, killing you instantly.

At least your friends were quick enough to avoid death.

THE END

Thanks to you, the bomb planted by "Henry," a spy for Imperial Japan, is deactivated. The spy is detained by military police in the brig until they figure out who he really is.

"Amazing job," your father says, beaming with pride. "But we have more work to do."

"Like what?" you say.

"Your mother and sister need our help."

You swallow nervously. "What happened?"

"They're missing," he says. "They might be walking to the hospital. Or they might be in trouble"

You nod.

➲ **GO TO PAGE 31.**

Japanese pilots continue to strafe the shipyard. You and Marvin bike-pedal from palm tree to structure to palm tree, staying out of sight.

You eventually reach the shoreline, handing over the manual to the crewmembers still struggling to free the men trapped inside the upside-down USS *Oklahoma*.

"Thanks, kid," says the lead rescuer. As he wades across the water to reach you on the beach you see he's covered in oil. "Any news?"

You nod. "Land invasion maybe," you say.

"Confirmed?" the man says, surprised.

You shake your head. "I heard it on the radio."

The man doesn't hear you. People are pleading for his help. "Good luck out there, kids," he says. He turns to head back to the capsized ship, then stops. "Wait," he says. "Take this."

It's a waterproof flashlight.

"Thanks," you say, pocketing it in your wet corduroy shorts.

➲ **SO NOW WHAT? DO YOU DECIDE TO JOIN YOUR FATHER IN STOPPING AN INVASION? IF SO, GO TO PAGE 66.**

➲ **AT SOME POINT, YOU NEED TO CHECK ON YOUR WOUNDED SISTER AND YOUR WORRIED MOTHER. TO HURRY HOME NOW, GO TO PAGE 83.**

You have secured the map of the USS *Oklahoma*. You step out of the ruined substation and immediately see a sailor running in the direction of Ford Island. He holds an off-its-hinge car door over his head. He uses the door as a shield from strafing.

"Sir, wait!" you yell.

The sailor stops, dropping the door. "Are you hurt?" he asks.

You shake your head. "Men are trapped in the *Oklahoma*," you say. "This document will show rescuers how to avoid blowing up the ship's fuel tanks."

"I'm headed there," the sailor says. "My brother is trapped in the hull. Let me take the map to the rescuers."

Trusting him, you hand it over.

The man says, "I owe you for this."

"I hope your brother is OK," you say.

He snaps to attention and salutes you. Then he picks up the car door again and runs in the direction of the ship.

You start to return the salute, but he's already gone. Then you and Marvin hop on your bikes, pedaling furiously to the beach.

"Can we make it in time?" Marvin asks.

"I hope so. I need to find my dad. My sister's hurt."

"We'll find him," Marvin says.

When you reach the jetty, the beach is deserted. A wedge-tailed shearwater dives for fish. The waves of Waikiki Beach are taller than you are. You're sweating furiously, but taking sips from Marvin's canteen keeps you hydrated.

You hear a noise, a puttering motor. Is it a submarine? If so, which direction is it coming from?

"Hide!" you say to Marvin.

The two of you push your bikes across the beach and into a cluster of golden cane palm. You survey the water.

"It's getting closer," you say.

"Let's leave!" Marvin says.

"Wait," you say, grabbing his arm.

Around the jetty, it arrives: a PT boat!

You sprint to the shoreline, waving your arms. "Dad!"

He stands proudly at the bow, waving back at you.

➲ **GO TO PAGE 17.**

You tell Henry to stop right there. You accuse him of working for the enemy.

"What are you talking about?" he says. "I'm here to fight the Imperial Army, not help them."

You shrug and start to walk away.

He suddenly lunges at you.

You dodge his attack. You push him back against the storage shed. He falls, slightly dazed.

⮕ **IF YOU GRAB HIS WALLET BEFORE TAKING OFF, GO TO PAGE 99.**

⮕ **IF YOU HIDE IN THE JUNGLE, GO TO PAGE 39.**

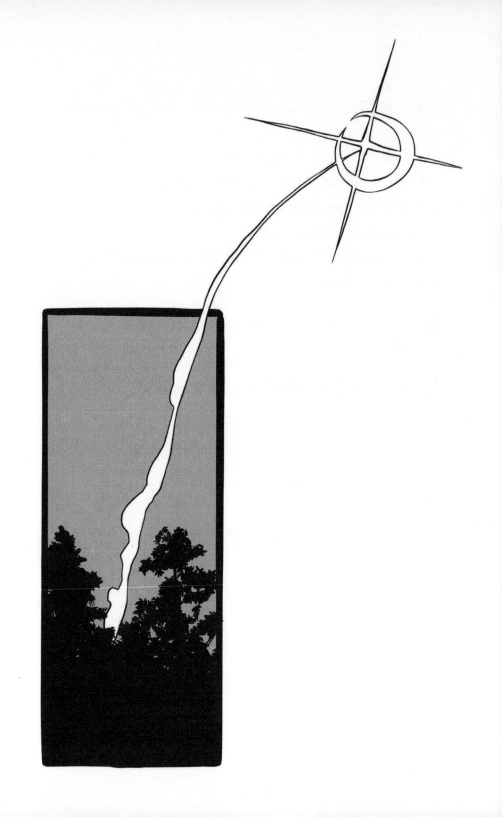

It works! The flare draws the attention of the enemy. He starts pursuing you through the jungle. You've saved the police officer from an ambush!

But you didn't think it through. What if the pilot captures you and the Kimura twins?

"Um, is there a plan here?" Don Kimura says.

You shrug and smile sheepishly.

The Kimura twins look at each other. Then they run ahead with Jenny. It dawns on you that the three of them were born on this island. They know the best hiding places. You moved here last year. Jenny and the Kimura twins are also great athletes, faster than anyone you know.

Can you escape this situation?

➲ **IF YOU TRY YOUR BEST TO KEEP UP WITH THE KIMURA TWINS, GO TO PAGE 106.**

➲ **IF YOU FIND YOUR OWN PLACE TO HIDE, GO TO PAGE 32.**

You follow the tracks. Jenny and the Kimura twins follow you. The prints lead to the edge of Ford Island. You see flattened sand, where a skiff was launched. And more boot marks.

Waipio Peninsula lies across the waterway. It's where tents are set up for soldiers during island-hopping missions in preparation for war.

It dawns on you that the Imperial Navy of Japan is going to use the U.S. island-hopping tactic to steal away your family!

"I—I don't know if I'm up for this," you say to Jenny.

She shakes her head. "We've come this far. We keep going."

"She's right," Dan Kimura says.

"You can do this," Don Kimura agrees.

Your friends believe in you, even if you don't believe in yourself.

You have the best friends in the world, you realize.

But do you have the courage of their conviction?

⮕ **TO FIND ANOTHER SKIFF TO REACH WAIPIO PENINSULA, GO TO PAGE 72.**

⮕ **TO BORROW YOUR FATHER'S MOTORCYCLE AND PURSUE THE KIDNAPPERS, GO TO PAGE 107.**

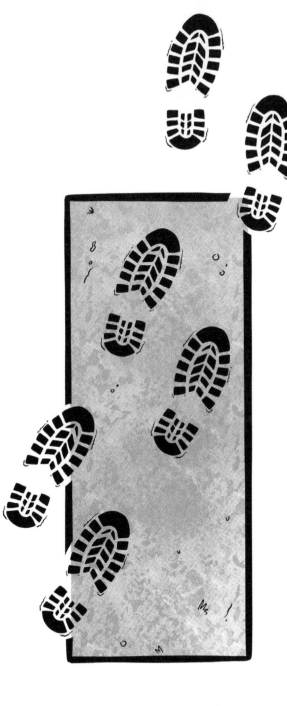

You won't let your classmates be thrown in jail just for having Japanese parents. You've stood beside them, hands over hearts, and pledged allegiance to the U.S. flag. You've sung "America the Beautiful" together. Heck, Jenny wrote your literature paper on Mark Twain in exchange for a stack of Captain America comics!

"Join me," you say, "in defending our island."

"You're not listening," says Jenny, flustered.

"I am. If we repel the attack, they can't imprison you. You can hide in plain sight."

She considers this, then looks at the Kimura twins. They shrug, then nod their heads.

"OK," she says. "How?"

"By flying a kite."

⮕ **TO USE A KITE TO SIGNAL A WARNING TO THE REMAINING SHIPS AT PEARL HARBOR, GO TO PAGE 79.**

⮕ **TO USE A KITE TO LURE JAPANESE PILOTS INTO AN AMBUSH, GO TO PAGE 45.**

You grab Henry's wallet and lockpick. Then you sprint, heading back through the jungle the same way you arrived.

You can hear Henry behind you, yelling for you to stop.

You trip on a rock and nearly knock yourself unconscious when you fall headfirst into a ravine. Water splashes your face. You scrape your hand on a rock.

You get up and trip over a cluster of hibiscus flowers.

Then you keep running.

➲ **GO TO PAGE 57.**

You and Beatrice race to the burning battleships. The *Oklahoma* is capsizing. Several other vessels are hit and smoking. Only the USS *Nevada* has started moving toward the channel.

The Imperial Navy of Japan is doing a number on this American naval base! You wish your friend Jenny was with you in this moment. She's a fun kid, wild at times. Jenny loves physical adventure. She told you yesterday that she was going fishing.

Sometimes you think you might have a crush on her.

Your friend Marvin is good at chess, smarter than anyone you know. You regret not dragging him along to find your father.

Given the ongoing air assault, it's unlikely you'll encounter a sailor who can take you to your dad's destroyer. But you have to try.

Before you see anyone from the base, something terrifying happens.

Out of nowhere, a badly damaged Zero fighter plane crashes into the water about 100 yards from the shoreline you're sprinting along.

You stop in your tracks. The pilot frantically struggles to slide open the glass cockpit and escape the sinking aircraft.

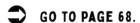 **GO TO PAGE 68.**

Pedaling back to the house with Marvin is tougher than you imagined. A bad idea, perhaps. After all, the roads are now badly damaged from Japanese bombs and antiaircraft shells. People keep stopping you to ask questions. Or to tell you that enemy soldiers are invading.

"I have to help my sister," you say. "Please let me through."

More disappointing is the fact that your dad sent you back with extra-strength aspirin. Your description of your sister's wounds didn't impress him.

The sky grows quiet. The air assault is over. You spent most of the last twenty minutes bicycling through chaos instead of helping.

When you finally get home, your sister is doing fine. Another doctor is there. Beatrice is bandaged. She smiles at you with a lollipop in her mouth.

"Where's your father?" your mother asks, distraught.

"I—I don't know."

You don't know what to say. Your father might be lost to you forever.

THE END

You secure the map and decide to take on the added responsibility of delivering the map of the ship. When you finally reach the rescue crew working to save the sailors trapped inside the USS *Oklahoma*, you accidentally slam your bike into an unexploded piece of ordnance.

You almost die for a reason, but the bomb is powerful.

The map is shredded into useless scraps.

THE END

You can only keep up with the Kimura twins for a minute. They're too fast, too strong. You whisper-scream their names—"Don and Dan, wait!"

Soon you're alone, running blindly through the jungle.

You're thirsty from exertion. You stop at a creek and cup water in your hands to drink. You hear a twig snap behind you.

No one addresses you. Still, you put your hands in the air and slowly turn around.

The man standing there isn't an enemy paratrooper.

He's a sailor in the U.S. Navy.

➲ **GO TO PAGE 48.**

You somehow remember how to kickstart your dad's Harley-Davidson. He only lets you drive it around the neighborhood. You know how to shift gears, sure. But you're not that experienced on it.

You wave goodbye to Jenny and the Kimura twins. Your stomach sinks with the possibility that this is the last time you see them.

Off you go, blasting the motorbike across a narrow bridge that leads to Waipio Peninsula.

You cross paths with U.S. security personnel in an armored car. You wave it down.

"My mom and sister have been kidnapped by Imperial Japan!"

The driver is an officer and laughs. Then he shakes his head. "We got them treated for minor injuries at the field hospital."

You look in the back seat, and there they are! Mom and Sis, bandaged but otherwise unharmed.

They scamper out of the car to give you the biggest hug.

You deactivated a bomb and found your family!

THE END

THE TRUE EVENTS BEHIND PEARL HARBOR

THE BACKDROP

Why did Imperial Japan attack the U.S. at Pearl Harbor? The reason was oil.

Imperial Japan wanted to build an empire, one that would rival Britain. However, Japan is an island, lacking the natural resources needed to flex its military might. At that time, Japan imported 94 percent of its oil.

The nation was already at war with China and desperately needed more resources to continue fighting. As a result, Japan occupied French Indochina—Vietnam, Laos, and Cambodia—in 1941. America froze all Japanese assets in the States and blockaded Japan from acquiring oil. Unwilling to submit to U.S demands, Japan plotted to take the oil by force.

Japan decided to attack the U.S Pacific Fleet at Pearl Harbor. The idea was that a savage attack would frighten the U.S. into negotiating for peace.

It was a gamble that didn't pay off. While the attack was an operational and tactical success, the strategy failed. The U.S didn't respond as hoped. Rather than embrace isolationism, the U.S. ramped up for war against both Japan and Germany.

THE NUMBERS

On Sunday December 7, 1941, the Imperial Japanese Navy attacked in two waves with:

- 6 aircraft carriers
- 408 airplanes
- 2 battleships
- 3 cruisers
- 9 destroyers
- 8 tankers
- 27 submarines

The Japanese lost twenty-nine aircraft and five submarines in the attack. One Japanese soldier was taken prisoner and 129 Japanese soldiers were killed. Of the Japanese ships that joined the Pearl Harbor assault, only one, the *Ushio* ("the Tide" in Japanese), made it to the end of the war.

THE TRUE STORY OF KAZUO SAKAMAKI, FIRST PRISONER OF WAR

Kazuo Sakamaki was one of ten sailors selected to attack Pearl Harbor in five midget submarines. Of the ten, nine died.

Sakamaki's submarine got stuck on a reef as it tried to enter Pearl Harbor. Sakamaki attempted to destroy the disabled submarine and swim ashore. However, the explosives failed to detonate. Sakamaki reached the beach, unconscious. Found by a U.S. soldier, he was arrested. He woke up in a hospital, the first Japanese prisoner of war held by the U.S. during World War II.

Sakamaki requested that he be allowed to kill himself, but the U.S. military refused to let him do this. He spent the rest of the war as a prisoner. Eventually, he returned to Japan, a pacifist.

For many years, he worked for the Toyota Motor Corporation. Sakamaki refused to talk about the war until 1991, when he attended a historical conference at the National Museum of the Pacific War in Fredericksburg, Texas. He cried when he saw his submarine on display at the museum for the first time in 50 years.

Sakamaki died in 1999 at the age of 81.

DECEMBER 7, 1941
PEARL HARBOR ATTACK TIMELINE
(HAWAII-ALEUTIAN TIME ZONE)

3:42 A.M. *Minesweeper USS* Condor *sights what is likely a submarine periscope near the entrance to Pearl Harbor.*

6:10 A.M. *First wave of 200 attack planes takes off from aircraft carriers assigned to the Imperial Japanese Navy's Pearl Harbor Strike Force, located 275 miles north of Oahu.*

6:45 A.M. *Destroyer USS* Ward *fires on a Japanese submarine, the first shots fired by the U.S. in WWII.*

6:53 A.M. *"We have attacked, fired upon, and dropped depth charges upon submarine operating in defensive sea area," Captain William W. Outerbridge announces over the radio. The submarine is destroyed, killing both Japanese crewmen inside. This is believed by U.S. servicemembers to be an isolated encounter, so no further action is taken.*

7:02 A.M. *U.S. Army radar operator spots unidentified aircraft racing toward the island.*

7:20 A.M. *U.S. Army lieutenant disregards the radar report, mistakenly convinced the formation is a cluster of air force bombers scheduled to arrive that morning.*

7:40 A.M. *Imperial Japanese aircraft reach Oahu.*

7:55 A.M. *Attack on Pearl Harbor begins.*

8:10 A.M. *Battleship USS* Arizona *explodes.*

8:17 A.M. *Destroyer USS* Helm *sinks a Japanese submarine at the harbor entrance.*

8:54 A.M. *Imperial Japan's second wave of aircraft, 170 planes, attacks.*

9:30 A.M. *Destroyer USS* Shaw *explodes in dry dock.*

10:00 A.M. *Japanese planes return to their carriers, ultimately returning to Japan.*

ZERO FIGHTER: AVIATION TRIUMPH

The Zero fighter plane, a.k.a. the Mitsubishi A6M, holds a major place in aviation history. Developed by Mitsubishi Heavy Industries in the 1930s, the Zero became Japan's most iconic and deadly aircraft during WWII.

The origins of the Zero can be traced back to the Imperial Japanese Navy's need for a carrier-based fighter plane. In 1937, Mitsubishi's chief engineer, Jiro Horikoshi, began designing the A6M. The Zero was noted for its maneuverability, range, and speed. Its lightweight construction allowed for increased agility. The aircraft had a powerful engine, reaching speeds beyond 300 m.p.h. The Zero had impressive range, too, dominating the Pacific skies.

The Zero made its combat debut in China in 1940. It proved its superiority over Allied aircraft with fearsome dogfighting capabilities. The Zero contributed to Japan's early victories.

As the war progressed, newer Allied aircraft offered improved weapons and performance. The American F6F Hellcat and F4U Corsair soon outpaced the Zero.

Despite its decline in effectiveness, the Zero is an enduring symbol of Japanese aviation. It revolutionized aerial warfare and set a benchmark for future fighter planes.

HIROSHIMA AND NAGASAKI: UNLEASHING UNPRECEDENTED DESTRUCTION

The bombings of Hiroshima and Nagasaki in August 1945 are etched in history. The tragedy of these detonations transformed warfare and global politics. These catastrophic events marked the first and only use of nuclear weapons in armed conflict.

Carried out by the U.S. on August 6, 1945, the "Little Boy" atomic bomb obliterated Hiroshima, instantly killing an estimated 70,000 people and decimating the city's infrastructure. Three days later, the "Fat Man" bomb devastated Nagasaki, claiming 40,000 lives.

Immeasurable suffering was inflicted on survivors, who endured physical injuries, trauma, and discrimination. Increased cancer rates, birth defects, and other health issues plagued the affected population for decades. These consequences underscore nuclear warfare's horrific toll.

The bombings of Hiroshima and Nagasaki altered the geopolitical landscape. They awakened people to the realization that humanity possesses the capacity to annihilate itself. This realization spurred efforts to control the proliferation of nuclear weapons and established organizations such as the United Nations and the Nuclear Non-Proliferation Treaty of 1968.

JAPANESE INTERNMENT CAMPS: A DARK CHAPTER

A repugnant outcome of the Japanese attack on Pearl Harbor was the establishment of Japanese internment camps. After Japan's attack on Pearl Harbor on December 7, 1941, fear and paranoia compelled the U.S. government to relocate and confine more than 120,000 Japanese-Americans living on the West Coast.

President Franklin D. Roosevelt signed Executive Order 9066 in February 1942, authorizing the internment of Japanese-Americans. This order led to the construction of camps in remote locations such as Manzanar and Tule Lake in California, and Heart Mountain in Wyoming. Given short notice to sell their belongings, Japanese-Americans were uprooted from their homes and extracted from their communities.

Life in the internment camps was marked by hardship and deprivation. Families lived in cramped barracks, lacking privacy and basic amenities. Internees faced challenges: limited healthcare, poor education, and meager job opportunities. Still, many Japanese-Americans successfully established schools and gardens inside the camps.

After the war, many struggled to rebuild their lives. The experience instilled a deep sense of anger in Japanese-

Americans. In 1988, the U.S. government formally apologized for the internment and provided reparations to surviving former internees.

The Japanese internment camps remind us of the consequences of fear, prejudice, and the erosion of civil liberties during war. Moreover, the internment camps remind us of the resilience of the Japanese-American community in the face of racism and government overreach.

JAPANESE STEREOTYPES IN WWII-ERA COMIC BOOKS

Popular culture often reflects the attitudes of its time. During WWII, comic books played a role in shaping public opinion. In their portrayal of Japanese characters, comics perpetuated harmful stereotypes that fueled discrimination.

WWII-era comics often depicted Japanese soldiers as ruthless, cunning, and inhuman. They were portrayed with exaggerated facial features, buckteeth, and slanted eyes, perpetuating a dehumanizing image that fed into the prevailing anti-Japanese sentiment. Japanese characters were frequently depicted as spies, saboteurs, or fanatical enemies. These portrayals reinforced negative stereotypes, fostering fear and mistrust among the American public.

The rich, diverse heritage of Japan was reduced to caricatures, distorting their customs, clothing, and way of life. These stereotypes had consequences. They contributed to the discrimination faced by Japanese Americans who were unjustly interned during WWII.

NANKING MASSACRE: HISTORICAL TRAGEDY

The Japanese invasion of China, particularly the occupation of Nanking, was a tragic chapter in history, marking the collective memory of both nations.

The invasion began in 1937, as Japanese forces advanced toward the city of Nanking, the capital of the Republic of China at the time. The occupation of Nanking led to widespread violence committed by Japanese soldiers against civilians and surrendered Chinese soldiers. Tens of thousands of Chinese civilians were killed. Countless others were tortured.

The Nanking Massacre is an example of inhumanity unleashed in war. Eyewitness accounts depict a chilling picture of violence, including mass executions.

Efforts to reconcile historical grievances continue, including memorial ceremonies and educational initiatives. Wounds inflicted during that period are deep, however. The healing continues.

SELECT BIBLIOGRAPHY

BOOKS AND ARTICLES

Burtness, Paul S., and Warren U. Ober. "Communication Lapses Leading to the Pearl Harbor Disaster." *The Historian* 75, no. 4 (2013): 740–59. http://www.jstor.org/stable/24456182.

Carroll D. Alcott. "Why Remember Pearl Harbor?" *The Antioch Review* 2, no. 1 (1942): 6–26. https://doi.org/10.2307/4608862.

Daniels, Roger. "Incarceration of the Japanese Americans: A Sixty-Year Perspective." *The History Teacher* 35, no. 3 (2002): 297–310. https://doi.org/10.2307/3054440.

"December 7th (long version)" US National Archives, Youtube, 2014, https://www.youtube.com/watch?v=gb7XUDlhz6k.

Entrikin, Helen. "Chapter 1. Pearl Harbor, Hawaii 7 December 1941 7:55 A.M: 'Like rats in a trap.'" *No Time for Fear: Voices of American Military Nurses in World War II*. East Lansing, Michigan: Michigan State University Press, 1996.

"Examine the facts and timeline of the Attack on Pearl Harbor on December 7, 1941." *Encyclopedia Britannica*, https://www.britannica.com/study/timeline-of-the-attack-on-pearl-harbor.

Gompert, David C., Hans Binnendijk, and Bonny Lin. "Japan's Attack on Pearl Harbor, 1941." In *Blinders, Blunders, and Wars: What America and China Can Learn*, 93–106. RAND Corporation, 2014. http://www.jstor.org/stable/10.7249/j.ctt1287m9t.15.

"How long did the Pearl Harbor attack last?." *Encyclopedia Britannica*, December 7, 2021. https://www.britannica.com/question/How-long-did-the-Pearl-Harbor-attack-last.

Lambert, Jack. "Pearl Harbor Revisited." *Air Power History* 37, no. 2 (1990): 37–40. http://www.jstor.org/stable/26271116.

Lord, Walter. *Day of Infamy.* [50th anniversary ed.]. New York: H. Holt, 1991.

Murphy, Larry. "Preservation at Pearl Harbor." *APT Bulletin: The Journal of Preservation Technology* 19, no. 1 (1987): 10–15. https://doi.org/10.2307/1494170.

"The Nurses' Contribution to American Victory: Facts and Figures from Pearl Harbor to V-J Day." *The American Journal of Nursing* 45, no. 9 (1945): 683–86. https://doi.org/10.2307/3416609.

Shurr, Agnes. "Chapter 1. Pearl Harbor, Hawaii 7 December 1941 7:55 A.M: 'Like rats in a trap.' " No Time for Fear: Voices of American Military Nurses in World War II. East Lansing, Michigan: Michigan State University Press, 1996.

Terrell Rickert, Lenore. "Chapter 1. Pearl Harbor, Hawaii 7 December 1941 7:55 A.M: 'Like rats in a trap.' " No Time for Fear: Voices of American Military Nurses in World War II. East Lansing, Michigan: Michigan State University Press, 1996.

Tyrrell, Tara. "The Women of Pearl Harbor." PearlHarbor.org, October 17, 2016, https://pearlharbor.org/women-pearl-harbor/

Veronico, Nick. *Pearl Harbor Air Raid: The Japanese Attack on the U.S. Pacific Fleet, December 7, 1941.* Guilford, Connecticut: Stackpole Books, 2017.

Wartime Heritage Association. "Major Annie Gayton Fox: United States Army Nurse Corps." Wartime Heritage Association, http://www.wartimeheritage.com/storyarchive2/story_annie_fox_us_army_nurse.htm

Zimm, Alan D. *Attack on Pearl Harbor Strategy, Combat, Myths, Deceptions.* Philadelphia, Pennsylvania: Casemate, 2011.

WEBSITES

www.75thwwiicommemoration.org/pearl-harbor-historic-sites
www.archives.gov/news/topics/remembering-pearl-harbor
www.nationalww2museum.org/war/topics/pearl-harbor-december-7-1941
www.nps.gov/perl/index.htm
www.pearlharborhistoricsites.org

ABOUT THE CREATORS

JARRET KEENE is an assistant professor in the English department at the University of Nevada, Las Vegas, where he teaches American literature and the graphic novel. He has written books, travel guide, rock-band biography, poetry collections, and edited short-fiction anthologies. His YA dystopian novel *Hammer of the Dogs* has been featured in *Writer's Digest* and *Publishers Weekly*. His books for Bushel & Peck Books include *Heroes of World War II* and *Decide & Survive: The Attack on Pearl Harbor*.

MIKE ANDERSON is a comic book artist, illustrator, and animator. A proud husband, father, and year-long Halloweener, Mike loves pizza to an indecent degree. Some of his clients include Scholastic, Subway, and Walmart, among others.

MILK & COOKIES is the middle-grade imprint of Bushel & Peck Books, a children's publisher with a special mission. Through our Book-for-Book Promise™, we donate one book to kids in need for every book we sell. Our beautiful books are given to kids through schools, libraries, local neighborhoods, shelters, and nonprofits, and also to many selfless organizations that are working hard to make a difference. So thank you for purchasing this book! Because of you, another book will make its way into the hands of a child who needs it most. Do you know a school, a library, or an organization that could use some free books for their kids? We'd love to help! Please fill out the nomination form on our website, and we'll do everything we can to make something happen.